Phoebe Flower's Adventures:

That's What Kids Are For

By Barbara A. Roberts

Illustrated by Kate Sternberg

ADVANTAGE BOOKS

Published by Advantage Books
4400 East-West Hwy., Suite 816
Bethesda, MD 20814-9393

Roberts, Barbara A., 1947–
    Phoebe Flower's adventures : that's what kids are for /
by Barbara A. Roberts ; illustrations by Kate Sternberg.
        p. cm. — (Phoebe Flower's adventures)
    Summary: As she starts second grade, impulsive Phoebe is sure that she will not be happy.
    ISBN 0-9660366-2-X
    [1. Schools—Fiction. 2. Behavior—Fiction.]
    I. Sternberg, Kate, 1954–   ill.   II. Title.
    III. Series: Roberts, Barbara A., 1947–   Phoebe Flower's adventures.
    PZ7.R5395Ph   1998
    [E]—dc21

                        10 9 8 7 6 5 4 3 2 1
                        Printed in the U.S.A.

12,253   pur 4/99

Contents

I would like to dedicate this book to my family
        Carly—my edification
        Nathan—my inspiritaion
        Megan—my visualization
        Michael—my foundation
Without their love and support this book would
not be possible.
And to my many friends who have encouraged me.
I would also like to give a special thanks to Suzanne—
my motivation.

                                        B.R.

        To Cozy & Beryl / Ken & Tom
                and
        My Sunrise Valley Family
                        K.S.

1

Don't Make Me, Please!

"Get up, get up, get up!" cries my mother as she kisses my forehead. "Today is the first day of second grade, Phoebe. You're going to love second grade. It was my favorite grade. You are really going to love it. I feel it in my heart. I just know it."

"Oh, ooh, no," I moan. "Don't make me get up. Please, don't make me. I won't like second grade. And worse than that, second grade won't like me. I couldn't even force myself to think about going to second grade this summer. I don't like school. I won't like second grade. I have no friends and I don't want any."

I slide underneath the covers, turn around so my head is at the bottom of my bed and put my feet on the pillows. "Tell my teacher you couldn't find me."

"But Phoebe, remember how we searched all over the mall for that perfect pair of faded blue jeans. Then we finally found them and I bought them for you even though they cost me way too much money? Remember you couldn't wait to wear them, but you knew they were too perfect to wear for just any old day? Those faded blue jeans have been waiting in your closet for the first day of second grade," explains my mother. "Hurry and get up. Put on those new faded blue jeans and make them happy. They have been waiting for this day. Hurry, Phoebe, the bus will be here very soon."

I drag myself out of bed, look in the mirror at a very sad second grade face, and yell, "Okay, I'll make those faded blue jeans

happy. I'll go to school and I'll show everybody that I was right. Second grade will not like me."

I pull on my new faded blue jeans, and my brand new dinosaur tee shirt. Then I drag myself down the hall to the breakfast table. I sit staring at my plate. "What are these two yellow eyeballs doing on my plate?" I ask.

"I always make fried eggs on the first day of school. Do you want jelly on your toast?" my mother asks me. "By the way, Phoebe, Amanda already ate her breakfast and . . . her bus comes fifteen minutes after yours. She loved her eggs. She wants me to make them every day."

Amanda is my older sister and, of course, she already ate her breakfast. She always does what she's supposed to do. In a word . . . Amanda is perfect. She's thirteen, sort of pretty, I guess, and everybody thinks she's brilliant, except me. I think she's a royal pain in the neck. She will make a great mother, someday, that's for sure, because she's had a lot of practice. She thinks she's thirty-two years old.

"Don't you remember the last time I tried to eat a fried egg and the egg got caught in the back of my throat and I couldn't swallow and I thought I would choke and die?" I ask. No one answers.

I try again. "How can anyone eat on the first day of school?"

Amanda looks at me and smiles like a thirty-two year old mother and says, "A good hearty breakfast is necessary for your brain, Phoebe. And, by the way, I think you should be more dressed up. You should definitely wear a skirt on the first day of school."

I don't know why I ever talk to her.

"How come Walter gets to eat oatmeal for breakfast?" I ask my mom. Walter is my baby brother. He has oatmeal all over his face. He's two years old and I know he likes me. When I make a funny face he laughs at me and says, "Up, Fee Fee. Up, Fee Fee." Then I pick him up and make more funny faces.

"Babies eat oatmeal, Phoebe, and don't worry about Walter. Worry about yourself. Are you finished with breakfast?" asks my mother. "R.V. is already on the corner waiting for the school bus. It'll be coming any minute."

2
My Only Friend

R.V. is Robert Vaughn III. He lives across the street from me. I call him Robbie. His family and close friends call him R.V., but not me. I used to call him R. V. until one day my mother told me how Mr. and Mrs. Spencer, our neighbors who live next door, bought an R. V. and were going to California. I thought

Robbie's parents had sold him to the Spencers because they didn't have any kids. Then finally I asked my mom if she would ever sell me to the Spencers if they decided they wanted a girl and she said, "What on earth are you talking about?"

"Well, they bought Robbie, didn't they?" I asked. "He hasn't been in school for a week and you told me they bought R.V."

I don't think I ever saw my mother laugh so hard. "No, sweetie," my mom said, "R.V., oops, I mean Robbie, has the chicken pox and that's why he's been out of school. The Spencers bought a Recreational Vehicle. People call it an R. V. for short. It's a big camper that they can use to go camping. I would never sell you, Phoebe, not for all the money in the world."

Well, that was then, and this is now, and when my mom finds out how much second grade hates me she will probably sell me for an M & M.

"Phoebe, I am talking to you. Did you eat anything? The bus is coming very soon so please take a bite of toast and hurry up. I don't want to drive you to school on the first day,"

pleads my mom as she leans over the sink to look out the window for the bus.

"This is your last chance, Mom. I can stay home and help you vacuum and dust. I can polish your silverware. You know how you say you never get a chance to polish your silverware. When you want to use it for Thanksgiving you can't because it looks so yucky. What d'ya say?" I beg and fall to my knees.

"Goodbye, Phoebe," says Amanda, with a disgusting smile on her face.

"Kiss me goodbye, Phoebe," says my mother wrapping her arms around my neck and squeezing me so tight I can't talk. "Remember, I have a good feeling about second grade. It'll be a great year."

I grab my book bag and my lunch and head out the front door. "Yuck to second grade!" I say to Buddy Dog as I pat his head on the way out the door. "I wish I was a dog."

Buddy Dog stretches his hind legs and peeks up at me under his bushy bangs. "I'm sure he was thinking and I'm very glad I am a dog."

Mom was right, Robbie was on the corner

waiting for the school bus. He had on a brown tie and shiny brown shoes. Amanda must have called his mother and told her that Robbie should get dressed up on the first day of school. Robbie has bright red hair and lots of freckles. He's my only friend. I don't know if it's because he has no other friends or because he really likes me. He likes to pick up worms and he knows how to make the greatest snowmen.

"Hi, Robbie, how come you're at the bus stop so early?" I shout at him as I cross the street. "Don't tell me you want to go to school."

"Well, sort of, Phoebe," Robbie answers. "Summer was getting pretty boring and my mom says that second grade is the best grade of all. I hope we're in the same room."

"Nobody says summer is boring, Robbie. You must be getting the chicken pox again," I tell him, feeling annoyed that his mom said the same thing about second grade as my mom did. Was that just a "mom thing" to say?

3

A Bad Bus Day

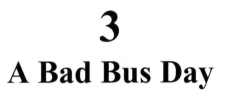

I see the bus coming around the corner. It pulls up and makes a loud sighing noise before it stops. The bus probably hates going to school, too. Robbie jumps on the bus first, runs down the aisle and sits in the farthest seat in the back. I start back there too. I like to sit in the back seat. No one can see me there and sometimes I wave and make faces at the cars behind the bus. When I find Robbie he smiles a "Sorry, Phoebe, there's no more room here," smile. "Just great," I think out loud, as I start to walk backwards up the aisle looking to the left and right, desperately trying to find somewhere to sit.

"Please take a seat!" the bus driver yells.

I'm almost back up to the front of the bus when I finally see an empty seat next to the window. "Could you please move over?" I say as nicely as I can to the curly haired girl sitting next to the empty seat.

"No!" she answers without looking at me.

"What's your name?" yells the bus driver.

"Phoebe," I whisper back. I feel my face getting hot.

"Well, Phoebe, sit down now!"

I climb over the curly haired girl and plop down just as the bus takes off.

"Phoebe, that's a funny name. How do you even spell it?" she says. "I have a beautiful name. My name is Elizabeth. And . . . didn't you know you should wear a skirt on the first day of school? I just moved here, and we would never wear dirty old jeans on the

first day of school."

My grandmother always says, "If you can't think of anything nice to say, don't say anything at all."

So the rest of the ride I don't say one word but I do think about my name. It is hard to spell and that's another reason I don't like school. I'd like to spell it FeeBee because that's alot easier to remember. I told my first grade teacher, Mrs. Ward, and she said "Now that you're in school, Phoebe, you have to spell your name the correct way. You don't want to start a bad habit do you?"

After what seems like a zillion days the bus door opens. I can finally get away from that awful Elizabeth. When I get off the bus, Robbie is nowhere to be found. I see a list in the hall that says, Phoebe Flower—room 24, teacher—Ms. Biz. My mother said she hoped I would get Ms. Biz because Mrs. Spencer's cousin's neighbor had her for second grade and she loved her. She said I would be very lucky to have Ms. Biz because she loves girls. I don't know if that's very lucky.

I have to go past my old first grade room to

get to room 24. Maybe I'll stop in and see Mrs. Ward, my first grade teacher, since I'm in no big hurry to meet Ms. Biz. I stick my head in and hear a voice say, "Hi, Phoebe! How was your summer?"

I answer, "Fine, thanks, Mrs. Ward."

"Want to come in and see the monarch chrysalis we have? Remember we had two last year and they changed into the most beautiful butterflies? Remember we let one go and had a freedom, farewell party? Remember we had butterfly crackers with orange marmalade and licorice to remind us of the color of the monarch butterfly?" Mrs. Ward asked.

"Sure," I answer, remembering that I dropped the spoon with the marmalade on my chair and then I sat on it. All day I stuck to every chair that I sat in.

Then Mrs. Ward asked, "Remember that one little girl in the class that couldn't stand to see those butterflies cooped up in the glass bottle and let one go in the classroom and it landed on top of the bookshelf and I had to get the custodian to get it down?" she asks.

"Sure," I said, realizing that Mrs. Ward

didn't remember that I was that little girl. "Well, I've got to go find my second grade classroom now. Good luck with those butter-flies, Mrs. Ward." I quickly skip out the door just as five new first graders are coming in. I squeeze out between them and continue down the hall looking for room 24.

4

So . . . This Is Second Grade

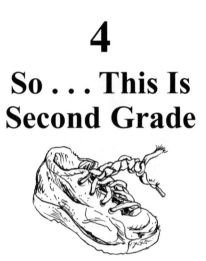

"Welcome!" cries a tall, skinny lady with short black hair standing in the doorway of room 24. "You must be Phoebe Flower. I'm Ms. Biz and we've been waiting for you. All the other boys and girls are here. Please find a seat and then we'll take attendance. I just love your jeans, Phoebe."

This might not be too bad. I look around to see who's in my class. Robbie is in the back of the room. He looks at me and waves a tiny wave and points to a seat next to him. Maybe my mom was right. Maybe second grade will be okay.

"Everyone is here today. Isn't that wonderful?" says Ms. Biz, "I love it when everyone is here. Owen, please pick someone to take the attendance slip to the health office with you."

"Elizabeth," says Owen.

Oh, rats, I didn't even see her. What a way to completely ruin a not-so-great day. She must have been sitting in the seat in front of Ms. Biz's desk.

"We will start today by having everyone tell us one thing they did over the summer. Who would like to begin?" Ms. Biz asks.

Four hands shot up in the air.

"I got a new puppy," says Evan, "and he's all mine. I'm in charge of training him."

"How responsible, Evan! Elaina?" asks Ms. Biz.

"I went to the creek with my brother and caught fourteen fish," Elaina says smiling at

My name is Ms. Biz
2nd grade
Social Studies
Math
Play
Science
lunch/Recess
P.E.
D.E.AR
How I spent my
Summer vacation
MS BIZ

Ms. Biz.

"Nice fishing, Elaina! Oh, and I just love the way Owen and Elizabeth walk quietly back from the office and sit down in their seats without a sound." Ms. Biz looks up and smiles at Elizabeth and Owen.

"Jeremy?" Ms. Biz continues to ask about vacations.

"I made a volcano out of soap suds and vinegar and I brought it in to show the class," said Jeremy, "but I'll need some help with it."

"Okay, Jeremy, pick a friend to help you," says Ms. Biz.

"Elizabeth, will you?" asks Jeremy.

"Why do boys always pick the same girl?" I whisper to Robbie. "Elizabeth got picked to go to the health office. Elizabeth, Elizabeth, Elizabeth, yuck!"

"Do you want to share something with the class, Phoebe?" Ms. Biz asks me.

"No thank you!" I answer. "I'm still thinking."

Second grade was just what I thought. I'm happy that Robbie's in my class, but mad as heck that Elizabeth is too. Not only do all the boys like Elizabeth, but so does Ms. Biz.

I can tell already that it will be "Elizabeth this" and "Elizabeth that" all year.

When it was my turn to tell about my summer vacation, I said, "I spent a week with my dad."

"Big deal," Elizabeth turned around in her seat and whispered, "I spend every day with my dad."

I couldn't wait to go home. I missed fifteen minutes of play time because I didn't finish my math. I didn't finish it for two reasons. One reason was I simply hate math. I just don't get it. Just because there were only six problems to do didn't matter. It seemed like six hundred. The second reason was I happened to pick a wobbly desk to sit in and when I bent over to put a book under the wobble part of my desk I noticed my sneaker was untied so of course I had to tie it because I could trip and kill myself. Then as I was tying it I wondered how many times I could tie my sneaker until I ran out of shoe lace. I could tie it six times and still have a little shoe lace left. Ms. Biz didn't care. She said, "Phoebe, you cannot go outside for playtime if your math isn't finished. I don't care how many times

you tied your sneaker."

My first day in second grade is almost over. I start to count the minutes until the bus will come and take me home. Finally, twelve minutes and thirteen seconds are left until the bell rings.

"May I have your attention?" Ms. Biz announces. "Over the summer, boys and girls, every teacher received two hundred dollars to spend on supplies for their classroom. I spent my money on entertainment. On the shelf you will find what you may think are toys, but I prefer to think of these items as entertainment. You will have ten minutes to look at the new items I purchased and tomorrow you will have more time to entertain yourself with them. Walk over to the shelves. Do not run, and please share."

5

That's Entertainment

Who cares? In about ten minutes and four seconds I'll be on the bus to home sweet home. I skip over to the shelf to have a look, anyway, just in case there's something good, but I doubt it. Robbie got to the shelf first.

"Hey, Robbie, what'd ya find to entertain with?" I ask him.

"This is so cool, Phoebe, it's a magnifying glass. Watch this!" he answers.

Robbie runs over to the fish bowl and covers his eye with the magnifying glass. "Look, there's no fish in here anymore. There are only whales." He runs to the gerbil cage. "Hey, everybody, come and look at the dinosaur." Robbie walks toward me and stares right at me for a long time. "Phoebe, you look so much older. You look like you're nine now, instead of eight."

"Let me see, let me see!" everyone yells at Robbie.

"Boys and girls!" calls Ms. Biz. "There is always tomorrow. It's time to get your book bags and line up to go home now."

Out of the corner of my eye, I see something red. I look again and can't believe it. Ms. Biz ordered an Etch-a-Sketch! I love Etch-a-Sketch. I had one when I was five and I could make the neatest house. I'll try it for just a minute. I grab it off the shelf and sit on the beanbag chair behind the bookshelf. I'll only be a minute. I just want to see if I can remember how to make a house.

Well, the next thing I remember is, "Phoebe

Flower, you missed your bus! What are you doing?" Ms. Biz was standing over me with a very red face. I could tell she was mad.

"Well, I saw this entertainment, Ms. Biz, and I thought I would just try to see if I could remember how to make a house like I did when I was five. I had an Etch-a-Sketch when I was five. I just had to put the roof on the house and then it would be finished. It was just going to be a minute." I try to explain.

"Phoebe, you missed your bus and now you have to go to the principal's office and she will have to call your mother to come and get you.

The principal will not be happy. Your mother will not be happy and I am not happy." Ms. Biz was talking pretty loudly.

"Sorry," I say, "but I only had to put the roof on." "Grab your book bag, Phoebe. Walk, do not skip, to the office and tell Dr. Nicely what happened," says Ms. Biz.

"Dr. Nicely, who's that?" I ask Ms. Biz.

"Dr. Nicely is our new principal, Phoebe, and like I said, Dr. Nicely will not be happy to have to call your mother on the first day of school."

I walk baby steps to the office. What's a doctor doing in school? I wonder. Maybe he'll take out my tonsils 'cause I missed the bus. Maybe he's a dentist. Maybe he pulls a tooth each time a kid misses the bus. Maybe I'll just run out the front door and never come back. I hear high heel footsteps coming down the hall. It has to be Ms. Biz coming to see if I went in the office yet. I push open the office door.

"Hi, Phoebe!" says Mrs. Walkerspeaking, the school secretary. I know her pretty well from last year. Robbie insists her name is just Mrs. Walker, but I know her better than he does

because I spent a lot of time in the office when I was in kindergarten and when I was in first grade. Every morning when she would get on the loud speaker she would say, "Good morning, this is Mrs. Walkerspeaking!" and every time she answered the telephone she would always say, "Hello, Mrs. Walkerspeaking."

"Hi," I mumble back.

"How's second grade going?" she asks.

"Do you know what an Etch-a-Sketch is, Mrs. Walkerspeaking? Well, I was just going to make a house like I did when I was five years old. I couldn't figure out how to put the roof on because triangles aren't easy to make. I didn't hear Ms. Biz. call my bus number. I was only going to be a minute and now Ms. Biz is mad at me and the Doctor is going to be mad at me and my mother is going to be mad and I'm going to have my teeth pulled out. I just want to go home."

"My name is Mrs. Walker, and yes, sure, I remember Etch-a-Sketch, Phoebe. I always had trouble with triangles too. Wait here," smiles Mrs. Walkerspeaking. "I'll go get Dr. Nicely."

I decided to go look in my book bag for an old cough drop. Maybe if I smell sick he'll feel sorry for me and won't pull my teeth. If he comes out of that office with plastic gloves and a white coat on, I am running out that door as fast as I can until I get to Alaska.

6
Dr. Who?

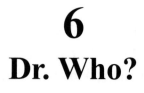

"Hello, Phoebe, I'm Dr. Nicely." says a voice that sounds like my Aunt Mary. I bite my lip hard so I won't cry and when I look up I see eyes that are the color of my favorite crayon, blue-green-purple. Dr. Nicely has on high heels and a blue-green-purple dress and blue-green-purple earrings. She looks like the lady that does the six o'clock news.

"Are you a doctor? Are you going to pull out my teeth?" I ask.

"No, Phoebe, I'm not going to pull your teeth. Come into my office and we'll talk." Dr. Nicely smiles.

"Well, I just want you to know I already told my mom that second grade wouldn't like me. She won't be surprised. It's not my fault. It really isn't. I didn't even want to be entertained. I just wanted to be home," I tell the doctor.

We walk together into Dr. Nicely's office.

"Are those all yours?" I ask pointing to the puppets lined up on the shelf over her desk.

"Yes, Phoebe, I collect puppets and marionettes," she answers. "Someday I'll come into your classroom and do a little show for your class and you can meet some of my friends on the shelf. Now, tell me why you missed your bus."

"Well . . . do you know what an Etch-a-Sketch is? Well . . . I just wanted to see if I could make a house like I did when I was five. I remember that I made a good house when I was five and I was just going to be a minute, but then I couldn't figure out how to make the roof. Even Mrs. Walkerspeaking knows that roofs are hard to make. She said she always had trouble with roofs. Anyway, I kept getting all messed up and I was only going to be a minute and I didn't hear Ms. Biz call my bus and now she is mad and my mother will be mad and you're going to pull out my teeth and I'm going to run away to Alaska," I say in one breath.

"I had an Etch-a-Sketch, too, Phoebe, and I was awful at making houses. My sister, though, she could make everything. She could make people with round heads. She could even write her name in cursive in a straight line." Dr. Nicely whispers to me, "If I tell you a secret, will you promise not to tell anyone?"

I look straight into those blue-green-violet eyes and answer, "I promise on a cross-my-heart. I will never, not even if someone pulls out all my teeth, Dr. Nicely. It will be our secret until death," I bravely tell her.

"Well, one day my sister made an Etch-a-Sketch picture of the whole family. She made arms and legs and fingers and toes. It was a real beauty. Then when I saw my sister go

DR. NICELY · principal

into the bathroom, I snuck into her room and shook the picture until it was gone. She never knew I did it." Dr. Nicely sighs.

"Wow!" I breathe. "Was she sad?"

"Oh, sure, and I felt terrible after I shook it but I was so jealous that I couldn't do Etch-a-Sketch like she could," Dr. Nicely says with a very sad face. "Remember Phoebe, this is our secret.'

"For sure, Dr. Nicely, for sure," I promise.

"And, I understand why you missed your bus, Phoebe," says Dr. Nicely, "but I will have to call your mother to come and pick you up and she will be not be happy. Does your mother work, Phoebe?"

"Yes, she brushes people's teeth at the dentist office, but she makes me brush my own," I explain.

"Well, you'll have to wait out in the office with Mrs. Walker until your mother comes, Phoebe, and give her this note. Keep practicing that Etch-a-Sketch, too, but please listen when your teacher calls the buses." Dr. Nicely sounds serious, but she still smiles at me.

I had to wait a half hour for my mom to come and pick me up. Ms. Biz was right. My mother was not happy. In fact, she didn't say one word until we got home. She opened the note that Dr. Nicely gave me and I could tell my mother didn't really care that much about my Etch-a-Sketch problem. "Don't let this happen again, Phoebe. I'll lose my job if I have to leave work early again."

For the next two days I tried so hard to be good at school. Ms. Biz actually asked me to take a message to the library and I made sure I walked straight there and straight back.

7

Rainbow Feet and
Toilet Fish

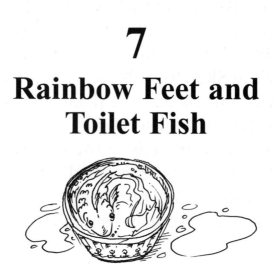

Then on the third day . . .

"Please, Phoebe, not another note from school!" says my mother. "I am very upset!"

"But Mom, I try to be good," I answer.

"I know you try, Phoebe, but today's note says, "Dear Mrs. Flower, Phoebe got into trouble today. She walked on the paintings that were drying in the hall and then continued to walk down the hall leaving blue and purple footprints zigzagging all the way to the library. Please speak to her about her behavior," Mother reads.

"But, Mom, let me explain what really happened," I moan.

"What happened then, Phoebe?" asks my mom, as she sinks into her chair.

"Well, Elaina was line leader of the week. She forgot to take the note the teacher told her to take to give to the librarian, so I hurried to the front of the line to remind her. I said, very politely of course, "Excuse me, Elaina, you forgot the note you were supposed to take," and Elaina thought I was budging her. She ignored me, so I had to move out into the hall to show her that I was trying to help her. Of course I didn't know that wet painted pictures were in the hall so I stepped on them. I didn't know that there was paint on my shoes when I walked down the hall to the library either." I stop to take a breath.

"Well, that makes sense, Phoebe," says my mother, "but please think about what you are doing. "

"Listen, Phoebe," said Amanda, as she walked into the living room from the kitchen, "I didn't mean to overhear your problem, but I did. Here's just a little lesson from your big sister. You should have minded your own business. Let Ms. Biz tell Elaina what to do. That's what teachers are for, you know."

I sigh. Sometimes I really don't like my sister and I really hate school. I've only made one other friend than Robbie and that's Jack, the class gerbil. I'm the only one who can feed Jack from my hand. The other kids are afraid of Jack and Jack seems to know I'm not. At bedtime after my mom puts Walter to bed, she comes into my room and hugs me. "I love you, Phoebe," she says. "Please try not to get in trouble at school tomorrow."

"Don't worry," I promise, "from now on, no more notes."

Two days later . . .

"I thought you said no more notes, Phoebe," my mother says. "What does this one say?" "Dear Mrs. Flower, Phoebe got into trouble today. She put our class goldfish in the toilet bowl. I am very surprised, as she is so kind to our gerbil, Jack. In fact, Phoebe is the only

one who can feed Jack from her hand. Phoebe needs to think about her behavior. Please speak to her!"

My eyes fill with tears as I say, "But, Mom, let me explain what really happened."

"What really happened, Phoebe?" asks my mom, as she plops deep into her chair.

"Well, I didn't know that the teacher was cleaning the fish tank and, of course, I asked why this fish was in a little paper cup and, of course, no one answered me because no one likes me except Jack, so I took that fish in that little paper cup, and I said to myself I am going to give that fish some room to swim, so I put that fish in the toilet bowl so he could have some room to really swim around." I pause.

"I am trying to understand, Phoebe, but you need to go to your room and think about what you did," says my mother. "And please, NO MORE NOTES FROM SCHOOL!"

I run to my room and throw myself on my bed. "School stinks" I say over and over again. I can't wait until I'm a grown-up and never have to go to school again.

I hear a knock as my bedroom door pushes open. "Phoebe, it's me," says Amanda. "I really didn't mean to eavesdrop, but I heard Mom yell at you. This is just a little big-sisterly advice. Let Ms. Biz clean the fish bowl by herself. That's what teachers are for, you know."

"Get out of my room, Amanda," I tell her as my eyes fill up with tears.

We eat dinner without saying much to each other. Walter tries to make us laugh by making funny noises, but Amanda tells him not to make noises with his mouth full. At bedtime, after my mother puts Walter to bed, she comes into my room and rocks me in her arms and sings her favorite songs. "Don't worry, Mom," I say, yawning. "This time, I promise, no more notes."

8
That's What Kids Are For

The very next day . . .

"Phoebe, you said, no more notes. YOU PROMISED, NO MORE NOTES," loudly moans my mother. "This note says. 'Dear Mrs. Flower, PHOEBE GOT INTO BIG TROUBLE TODAY! SHE DIDN'T SIT AT HER DESK. SHE SAT UNDER IT WITH HER FEET ON THE SEAT. SHE DIDN'T

WRITE HER NAME ON HER PAPER. SHE DREW HER PICTURE INSTEAD. Phoebe needs to think about her behavior. Please speak to her.'" My mother crumples up the note and throws it in the basket.

"That's it!! No more T.V.! No more ANY-THING!" cries my mother.

"But Mom, let me tell you what really happened," I cry. "What really happened then, Phoebe?" says my mother, looking totally exhausted as she fell into the chair.

"Well, Robbie wanted to borrow my pencil and the point was pretty dull, so I raised my hand to ask Ms. Biz if I could sharpen it. Of course, she didn't see me, so I looked in my desk for a sharp pencil and I couldn't find one. I had to sit on the floor to get a better look into my desk and then I got tired. I wanted to put my feet up and there was nowhere to put my feet except on my chair. No one would have known, except Elizabeth had to tell the teacher that I was sitting on the floor with my feet on the chair. Then, because I gave Robbie my only pencil, I couldn't write my name too well so I thought that I should draw my picture be-cause I draw my picture much better than I

47

write my name."

"I am trying to understand, Phoebe. I am trying really hard . . . but this time I mean it . . . not one more note," begs my mother. "Please think before you act."

"No more notes," I repeat. "This time I really truly promise."

I go outside and sit on the swing. Buddy dog bounces over and sniffs me. "I really don't mean to do these things, Buddy dog. I just forget. Then everybody always gets mad at me. Can I come and live in your doghouse with you?"

"Woof," barks Buddy dog.

"Phoebe," calls Amanda.

Oh great, a little sisterly advice, just what I want to hear, I think to myself. "I'm not here," I answer.

"Phoebe," Amanda walks over to the swing set and starts to speak, "just a little big-sisterly advice, next time tell Robbie to ask the teacher for a pencil. That's what teachers are for, you know."

"Thank you, Amanda, next time I will," I say staring right at her and remembering what my grandmother said about not saying

anything if you can't think of anything nice to
say.

At bedtime that night, my mother and I
snuggle together as we read a book. My
mother hugs me tightly and says, "I know you
have a hard time sitting still, Phoebe. I know
you don't always think before you do something. I really do understand. I didn't want to tell
you this, but I had a hard time in school too.
I used to say a little rhyme to myself when I
had trouble concentrating. It went like this:

Think, think
It's good for the brain.
And your teachers and friends
Won't think you're a pain.

Please try harder and remember I love you very much."

"Thanks, Mom, I'll try that," I say. "I love you too!"

One week later . . . "Oh no! I knew it was too good to be true. It's been a whole week without a note, Phoebe," says my mother. Slowly, very slowly, my mom opens the note. "Dear Mrs. Flower," she reads out loud. "Phoebe has had a great day."

"Today, Phoebe was a heroine. Robbie let Jack out of his cage. Jack jumped out of our window and ran across the playground toward the flagpole in the front of the school. Just as the custodian began to raise the flag for the day, Jack leaped onto the flag and his claws became stuck. The custodian didn't see him and Jack rode up to the top of the pole. Without thinking about it, Phoebe ran to the flagpole, shimmied up to the top, picked up Jack, put him on her shoulder, and slid back down. The whole class watched with amazement.

When Phoebe came down we all clapped for her wonderful rescue. You should be very proud of Phoebe."

"Phoebe, I am so proud of you," laughs my mother as she hugs me. "You are a true heroine."

"But Mom, let me tell you what really happened," I say.

"What really happened, Phoebe?" asks my mother.

"My teacher said I didn't think about it. I did think about it. I just wanted to save Jack." I smile and give my mother a big hug.

Then, as fast as I can, I leap up the stairs, two steps at a time, to Amanda's bedroom. I knock and open her bedroom door at the same time. "Amanda," I say, as I fold my arms across my chest, "just a little sisterly advice for my big sister. If you want to be a heroine, don't wait for the teacher to do it. That's what kids are for, you know."